The Gruffalo Winter Nature Trail

This book belongs to

Gruffalo Explorer

....

Step inside the deep dark wood and join the Gruffalo
and the Gruffalo's Child for a fun family nature trail.

To be a true Gruffalo Nature Explorer, you'll need
to keep your eyes open and your ears to the ground
and don't forget to take this guide with you!
It's full of games, activities and hundreds of stickers
to keep you looking for and learning about nature.

Autumn is over and winter is here so
it's time wrap up and head outside . . .

Snow doesn't
count as
a hat!

I'd wear a hat if I were you

Winter Wonders

Icy puddle
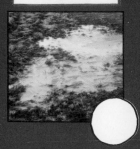

Holly and berries

Tree stump

Wriggly tree roots
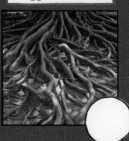

Robin

Dead leaves

Squirrel nests are called dreys!

Drey

Conifer

Old nest
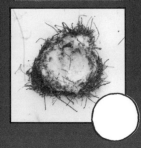

Snowflakes

Squirrel

Icicles

Look at all the wintry pictures below.
How many can you see on your stroll?
Put a Gruffalo paw sticker next to each one. →

Mistletoe

Feeding birds

Snowy footprints

Your footprints can be the first!

Nut

Moss

Green lichen

Snowy branch

Pine cone

Bare branches

A frosty leaf

A frosty web

Fresh snow

Fresh snow should be untouched by any foot

Snow Gruffalo

Decorate this snowy scene
and use your stickers to
build a snow gruffalo.

Aha! Oho! A trail in the snow!

The Gruffalo's Child sees three snowy tracks when she's out on her walk. Use your stickers to match the right animal to the right track.

Snake

Owl

Owl

Fox

Snake

Fox

Paw Prints

It's sometimes easier to see animal or human tracks in snow.
Look very carefully – how many of these can you see?
Put a Gruffalo paw sticker next to each one you spot.

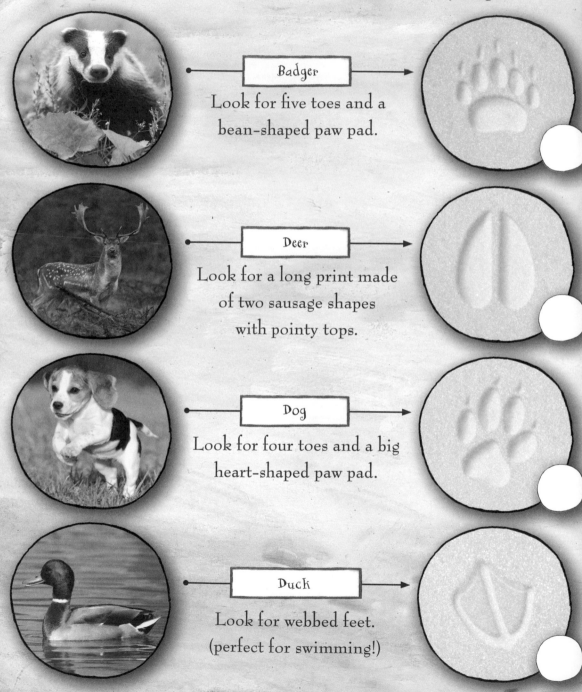

Badger

Look for five toes and a
bean-shaped paw pad.

Deer

Look for a long print made
of two sausage shapes
with pointy tops.

Dog

Look for four toes and a big
heart-shaped paw pad.

Duck

Look for webbed feet.
(perfect for swimming!)

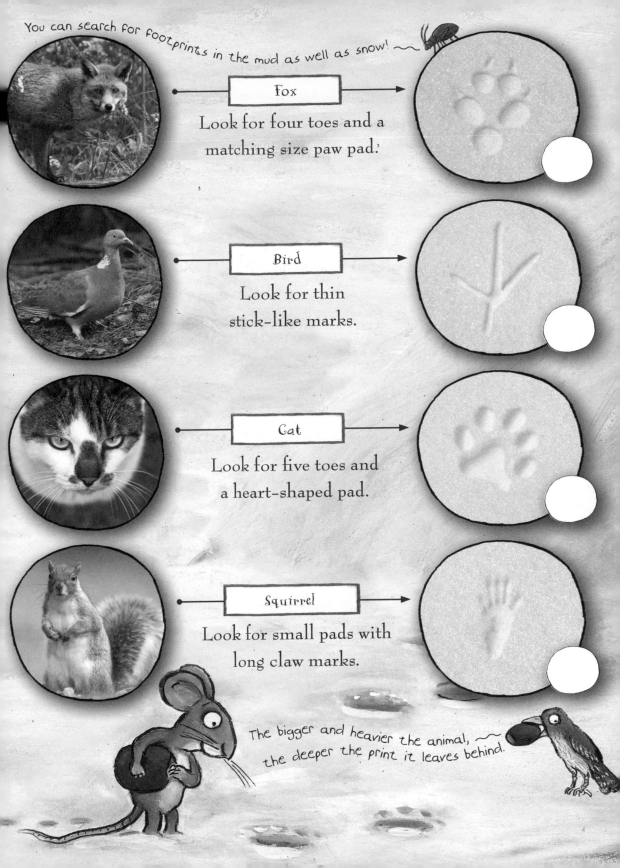

You can search for footprints in the mud as well as snow!

Fox

Look for four toes and a matching size paw pad.

Bird

Look for thin stick-like marks.

Cat

Look for five toes and a heart-shaped pad.

Squirrel

Look for small pads with long claw marks.

The bigger and heavier the animal, the deeper the print it leaves behind.

Animal Tracks

Fill this page with animal tracks! Tracks you've seen or maybe tracks you wish you'd seen. You can use pencils, crayons or maybe even thumbprints.

Tree Faces

Have you ever spotted a face in a tree?
The woods are full of them!

Keep your eyes peeled and see
how many you can spot on
your winter walk.

Who Made That Hole?

Have you ever seen a hole near a tree or in a bank and wondered who lives inside it? Winter is a good time to spot animal burrows or dens, where some animals eat, sleep and raise their offspring. The cold weather often means greenery has died away so you can see the hole clearly. Put a sticker next to each hole that you see.

Water vole

Burrow

Look for small holes in banks of land close to the water's edge. The grass will be shorter around the entrance to the hole.

Fox

Den

These are everywhere in the countryside! Look for food remains outside a single fox-sized entrance.

Mole

Hill

Look for small heaps of mud. Moles don't live in the mud mound, it's a sign that they have tunneled below!

Rabbit

Warren

Look for a rabbit-sized hole on slopes and banks with rabbit droppings near the entrance.

Cosy Cave

The Gruffalo and the Gruffalo's Child live inside a cave.
Use your stickers to decorate the inside of their home.

Where do they come from and where do they go?

The Gruffalo's Child follows the snowy tracks to find an animal, but where do the creatures below live? Use your stickers to match the right animal to the right home!

~ Who else do you think lives underground?

Winter Weather Watch

The snow fell fast and the wind blew wild . . .
What is the weather like today? Winter weather changes all the time.
Keep watch and add a sticker for each type of weather you experience!

Snow

Clouds

Clear blue sky

Wind

Fog

Storm

Grey sky

Rain

Hailstones

I'm so cold . . .

Make a Snow Scene

Why not make a pretty snow scene and create your own weather.

You will need:

A clean empty jar, scissors, desiccated coconut and glitter.
To make a nature snow globe you'll need a sponge, pine cones, dried leaves or twigs. To make a Gruffalo snow globe you'll need white, black and red modelling clay, tiny twigs and an adult to help you.

Nature snow globe:

Cut the sponge into a dome shape and glue inside the lid of your jar. If you would like your nature scene to sparkle just add small dots of glue to your twigs and leaves and sprinkle with glitter. Use your scissors to cut little slots into the sponge and when they are dry, press your leaves and twigs into the slots. Remember that your display needs to fit inside the jar, so don't make it too big!

Add two tablespoons of desiccated coconut and a teaspoon of glitter to your jar, then tightly screw the lid and the nature display into position.

Turn upside-down and enjoy your snow scene!

Always glue your displays in the centre of your jar lids. If they are too near the edge they may not fit inside the jar.

Gruffalo snow globe:

To make a snow gruffalo display, instead of a sponge you'll need white modelling clay.

1   **2**   **3**   **4**

Roll three balls of clay, with a fourth that's a bit bigger.
Glue the biggest ball inside the jar lid, keeping it away from the
edge of the lid, and leave to dry.

Push a twig through the three small balls,
leaving about 2cm at the bottom which
you push into the larger ball.

If you only have white modelling clay you can always
use paint to add the snow gruffalo's features!

Glue into position. When the glue
is dry you can then begin to shape
your snow gruffalo, by adding
eyes, teeth, ears, claws and horns.
Your tiny twigs make perfect
claws!

Make a Gruffalo Snowflake

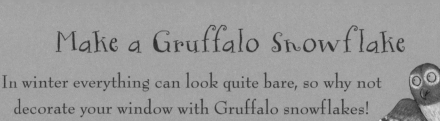

In winter everything can look quite bare, so why not decorate your window with Gruffalo snowflakes!

You will need:
A4 white paper, small scissors, a pencil, a black felt pen, a ruler, a paper clip, an empty cereal box and an adult to help you.

Start with a 21cm x 21cm square piece of paper. Fold corner to corner, like this.

You now have a triangle and you need to fold corner to corner. Do this twice.

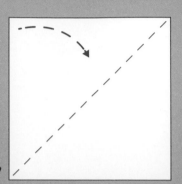

Folded edge

Trace this outline onto a piece of paper and glue the traced drawing to card (the back of a cereal packet will do!). Carefully cut away the blacked out areas. This is your template.

Place your triangle of paper here.

Make sure the folded edge is on the left! Now put your template on top and trace around it with your pencil. Cut away the black areas as shown.

Use a paper clip to hold the paper together whilst you trace around it and cut

Fold the face in half and
draw a semi-circle as shown.
Cut the semi-circle out – this
will make the Gruffalo's eyes!

Semi-circle

folded edge

You could draw his eyes
instead of cutting them

Now carefully unfold the snowflake,
tape it to a window and enjoy!

Hello Spider!

In winter when you're keeping warm inside your house, keep your eyes peeled for these eight legged house guests. Put a sticker next to each one you spot.

Cupboard spider

False widow spider

Cardinal spider

Giant house spider
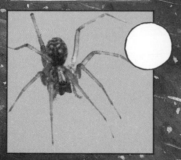

Zebra jumping spider

Tube spider

Cellar Spider

Missing sector orb weaver spider

This spider spins a web where one section is completely missing!

If you have seen a spider in your house,
then reward yourself with this badge! →
How big was it? Draw it here:

I've seen a spider!

Winter Birds

Some birds migrate in the winter.

Robin

Starling

Chaffinch

Greenfinch

Carrion crow

Magpie

Blackbird

House sparrow

Jay

Barn owl

Black swan

Greater spotted woodpecker

Migration means they fly off to warmer countries once it starts to get cold. But plenty of birds stay all year round. Which ones can you spot? Put a bird sticker next to each one.

Swan

Great tit

Collared dove

Wren

Jackdaw

Rook

Feral Pigeon

Wood Pigeon

Blue Tit

Winter is a great time to spot hungry birds looking for food. The bare branches make them easier to spot!

EXPERT EXPLORERS

Marsh tit

Coal tit

Green woodpecker

Make a Forest

You will need:

green paper, scissors, tape, glue, glitter, a pencil and an adult to help you.

Find something round, like a saucer or a cup, and place it onto your green paper. Use a pencil to trace around the object to create a circle shape, then cut out the circle and cut it in half as shown in the picture.

~ One circle will make two trees!

With the straight edge at the top, take each corner of your semi circle and curl them together until you've made a cone. Tape it together to make a basic tree shape.

Now for the leaves!

You can cut long strips of green paper as shown in the picture and make lots of thin cuts along the strip, being careful not to cut all the way to the top! Then cut three small triangle shapes along the top edge to help the paper curve around the tree.

Glue or tape along the top edge of the strip and stick into position on your tree, starting at the bottom and adding new strips of paper as you work your way up to the top!

~ Curve your leaves by wrapping them around a pencil!

You can also make leaves by cutting out small triangles of green paper. Use your pencil to curve the bottom of each leaf before gluing or taping them to the bottom of the tree.

Start at the bottom and work your way up – the bigger the tree the more leaves you will need! ↘

You can decorate some of your trees with glitter!

You can also add leaves by drawing them on. Use a colour pencil that's lighter or darker than the green of the tree to make sure they stand out.

~ If you cut out lots of different size circles you will end up with a forest full of different size trees!

Goodbye Winter!

Winter can feel long, but the weather will gradually feel warmer and many signs of spring will soon start to appear. Put a butterfly sticker next to each sign of spring you see.

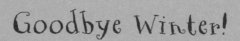

Frogspawn

Snowdrops

Buds

Blossom

Daffoldils

Primroses

Ducklings

Crocuses

Well done, you are now a
Gruffalo Explorer!

Reward yourself with a
special sticker like this

I'm a
Gruffalo
Explorer!

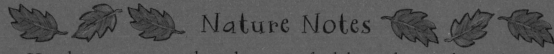

Nature Notes

Use these pages to stick in things you find, keep photos of your day or
write poems or stories about the things you have seen.

 Nature Notes

 Nature Notes

Nature Notes